FROSTY the SNOWMAN ™

By Diane Muldrow
Cover illustrated by Robbin Cuddy
Interior illustrated by Josie Yee

A GOLDEN BOOK • NEW YORK

Classic Media

TM & © 2001, 2013 Warner Bros. Entertainment Inc. & Classic Media, LLC.
Based on the musical composition FROSTY THE SNOWMAN © Warner/Chappell.
(s13)
RHUS29667

Published in the United States by Golden Books, an imprint of Random House Children's Books, a division of
Penguin Random House LLC, 1745 Broadway, New York, NY, 10019, and in Canada by Random House of Canada,
a division of Penguin Random House Ltd., Toronto. Originally published in slightly different form by
Golden Books in 2001. Golden Books, A Golden Book, A Little Golden Book, the G colophon, and the distinctive spine
design are registered trademarks of Penguin Random House LLC.
randomhousekids.com
ISBN 978-0-307-96038-2
Printed in the United States of America   19 18 17 16 15 14 13 12 11 10

It all started with the snow, the first snow of the season.

As every child knows, there's a certain magic to the very first snow.
And when it falls on the day before Christmas, something wonderful
is bound to happen!

"Children, back to your seats!" called the teacher. "The snow can wait. I've hired Professor Hinkle, the magician, to entertain us for our Christmas party!"

Unfortunately, Professor Hinkle was just about the worst magician in the world.

"And so I put the eggs into my magic
hat," said Professor Hinkle. "Abracadabra!
And *voilà*, the eggs have turned into . . . a mess.
Where is my rabbit?
Hocus Pocus, where are you?"
He didn't know that his rabbit,
Hocus Pocus, was hiding
in the hat.

"The only thing this hat is good for is the trash can!" said Professor Hinkle.

But the hat didn't stay in the trash for long. The hat—with Hocus Pocus underneath—hopped out the door! That was when the bell rang. The children were free for the whole Christmas holiday!

"Hey, look at the snow!" cried the children as they ran outside.
They worked together to build the first snowman of the season.

Once the children had given him eyes, a nose, and a mouth,
it was time to name him.

"How about Frosty?" asked Karen. "Frosty the Snowman!"

The children danced around Frosty as they sang about his button nose and his eyes made out of coal.

"Come back here, you!" cried Professor Hinkle, chasing Hocus Pocus. Suddenly, a gust of wind blew the hat onto Frosty's head!

"Happy Birthday!" said the snowman.

Karen gasped and said, "That hat brought Frosty to life. It must be magic!"

When Professor Hinkle heard that, he wanted the hat back!

"But it's not yours anymore," protested Karen.

"This hat will make me a millionaire!" said the greedy magician, taking the hat back.

Hocus Pocus felt that the hat really did belong to Frosty. So he hop, hop, hopped back to Frosty and the children as fast as he could to return the magic hat.

"Happy Birthday!" said Frosty again as soon as the hat
was placed on his head. "Hey, I said my first words. I'm alive!
What a neat thing to happen to a nice guy like me!"

The magic hat made Frosty dance around. The children cheered as Frosty began to laugh and play with them. There had never been such a wonderful winter day!

When the sun peeked out from
behind the clouds, Frosty exclaimed,
"Oh, I'm all wishy-washy! I'm starting to melt!"
The children knew they needed to take Frosty someplace
where he'd never melt — like the chilly North Pole. They decided to go to the
railroad station and find a train for Frosty.

"Let's have a parade through town!" shouted Frosty. "Come on, kids—
follow the leader!"

All too soon it was time for the train, and Frosty, to leave.

"I'll go with you, Frosty," said Karen. "I'm sure I'll be back in time for supper."

Karen, Frosty, and Hocus Pocus jumped into a refrigerated boxcar on a freight train headed north.

No one saw Professor Hinkle sneak under the train car and hold on.

A refrigerated boxcar is a splendid way to travel. Splendid, that is, if one is a snowman or a furry-coated rabbit. But for a little girl like Karen, it was just too cold.

So when the freight train made a stop, Frosty got them all out. No one saw Professor Hinkle jump off, too.

Frosty took Karen and Hocus Pocus to a wooded glen, where
they found animals decorating the trees for their big celebration.
They knew Santa Claus was coming that night!

After Hocus Pocus spoke to the animals, they agreed to build
a campfire to keep Karen warm.

But it didn't take long for Professor Hinkle to catch up with
the friends.

"Get on my shoulders, Karen!" cried Frosty.

Frosty, since he was made of snow, was the fastest belly whopper in the world. Soon he and Karen were sliding down a hill, leaving that greedy Professor Hinkle far behind.

At the bottom of the hill was a tiny greenhouse for growing tropical poinsettias for Christmas. It was the perfect place for Karen to stay warm.

"Frosty, you'll melt in here!" warned Karen.

"I'll only stay inside for a minute," Frosty assured her.

But that nasty Professor Hinkle caught up with them
once again. He locked the door, trapping the friends inside!

That night, Hocus Pocus led Santa Claus to the greenhouse
to save Frosty. But by then, poor Frosty had melted completely.

"Don't cry, Karen," said Santa kindly. "Frosty's not gone for
good. You see, he was made out of Christmas snow. You can bet
your boots that when a good, jolly December wind kisses it, it'll
turn into Christmas snow all over again. Just watch!"

Santa opened the door, and when the wind whirled in and
out, Frosty was back!

Santa was about to place the magic hat on Frosty's head when Professor Hinkle shouted, "I want that hat, and I want it now!"

Santa replied, "If you touch this hat, I'll never bring you another Christmas present. Go home right now and write 'I am very sorry for what I did to Frosty' a hundred zillion times. Then maybe, just maybe, you'll find something in your stocking tomorrow morning."

Professor Hinkle was very sorry indeed. He ran straight home to start writing.

"Happy Birthday!" said Frosty once more.

Karen was happy to see her friend again. But now it was time to go home. Santa put Karen in his sleigh and promised her that he would take Frosty back to the North Pole with him.

Karen hated to say good-bye to Frosty, but Santa said that
Frosty could return every year with the magical Christmas snow.

Frosty waved good-bye as he hurried on his way. He shouted
a promise to return the following Christmas. And every year,
he did just that!

Merry Christmas!